97

DATE DUE

NOISY NORA

WITH ALL NEW ILLUSTRATIONS

▶ROSEMARY WELLS◀

DIAL BOOKS FOR YOUNG READERS
NEW YORK

Published by Dial Books for Young Readers
A Division of Penguin Books USA Inc.
375 Hudson Street
New York, New York 10014

Text copyright © 1973 by Rosemary Wells
Illustrations completely redrawn copyright © 1997 by Rosemary Wells
All rights reserved
Designed by Julie Rauer
Printed in the U.S.A.
First Edition
1 3 5 7 9 10 8 6 4 2

Library of Congress Cataloging in Publication Data
Wells, Rosemary.
Noisy Nora / with all new illustrations / Rosemary Wells.—1st ed.
p. cm.
Summary: Feeling neglected, Nora makes more and
more noise to attract her parents' attention.
ISBN 0-8037-1835-7 (trade) ISBN 0-8037-1836-5 (lib. bdg.)
[1. Behavior—Fiction. 2. Family life—Fiction. 3. Stories in rhyme.] I. Title.
PZ8.3.W465No 1997 [E]—dc20 96-4275 CIP AC

The art is all new pen-and-ink drawings with watercolor, gouache,
acrylic ink, india ink, colored pencil, and pastel.

for Joan Read

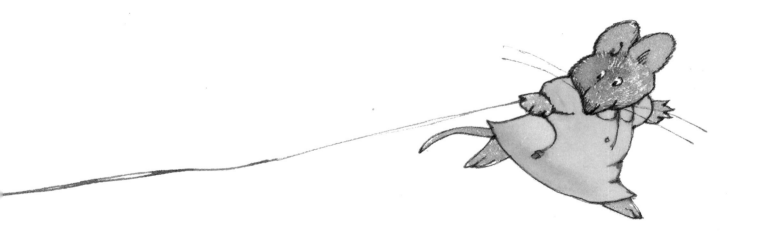

Jack had dinner early,

Father played with Kate,

Jack needed burping,
So Nora had to wait.

First she banged the window,

Then she slammed the door,

Then she dropped her sister's marbles
on the kitchen floor.

"Quiet!" said her father.
"Hush!" said her mum.

"Nora!" said her sister,
"Why are you so dumb?"

Jack had gotten filthy,

Mother cooked with Kate,

Jack needed drying off,
So Nora had to wait.

First she knocked the lamp down,
Then she felled some chairs,

Then she took her brother's kite

And flew it down the stairs.

"Quiet!" said her father.
"Hush!" said her mum.

"Nora!" said her sister,
"Why are you so dumb?"

Jack was getting sleepy,

Father read with Kate,

Jack needed singing to,
So Nora had to wait.

"I'm leaving!" shouted Nora,
"And I'm never coming back!"

And they didn't hear a sound
But a tralala from Jack.

Father stopped his reading.
Mother stopped her song.

"Mercy!" said her sister,
"Something's very wrong."

No Nora in the cellar.
No Nora in the tub.

No Nora in the mailbox
Or hiding in a shrub.

"She's left us!" moaned her mother
As they sifted through the trash.

"But I'm back again!" said Nora

With a monumental crash.